VOYAGE
OF THE
HALF MOON

by Tracey West

SILVER MOON PRESS
NEW YORK

VOYAGE OF THE HALF MOON
by Tracey West
Copyright © 1993 by Kaleidoscope Press

For information contact
Silver Moon Press
New York, New York
(800) 874-3320

Designed by John J. H. Kim
Cover Illustration by Nan Golub
Printed in the United States of America

Library of Congress Cataloging-in-Publication Data

West, Tracey
    Voyage of the Half Moon
    p. cm. -- (Stories of the States)
    Includes bibliographical references (p. 88)
    Summary: A fictionalized account of Henry Hudson's third attempt to find the Northwest Passage, sailing up what will come to be known as the Hudson River, accompanied by his twelve-year-old son.
ISBN 1-881889-18-1 (hardcover): $13.95
ISBN 1-881889-76-9 (paperback): $5.95
1. Hudson, Henry, d. 1611--Juvenile Fiction.
[1.Hudson, Henry, d. 1611-Fiction. 2. American--Discovery and exploration--Fiction.] I. Title. II. Series.
PZ7.W51937Vo 1993
[Fic]--dc20

                                        93-16462
                                            CIP
                                            AC

STORIES OF THE STATES

TABLE OF CONTENTS

CHAPTER ONE
"The New World"

"Help us! Help us!" John Hudson looked up, startled, when he heard the anguished cry. He peered over the rail of the *Half Moon* and saw a rowboat approaching.

"Help us!" came the cry again. John could see the men frantically rowing their boat to the larger ship. His heart sank.

Henry Hudson ran from the ship's bow to greet the approaching boat. John followed.

"Father, what's happened?" John asked. Captain Hudson turned and pushed John back. As he turned away, John caught a glimpse of the small craft. Its bow was awash with blood.

"It looks as if the men were attacked," Hudson said grimly.

"Who would attack the men?" John asked, pain and confusion in his voice.

"It must have been the native people of this land," Henry Hudson explained. He leaned over the railing and called out, "Was anyone seriously hurt?"

"Aye, sir," one man wailed. "It's John Colman. An arrow pierced his neck. He's dead, sir — dead and gone!"

John put his hand to his own neck and felt a lump form in his throat. Colman had been his friend. He had taught John how to tie the knots he had just been practicing.

John Hudson had gone on his first exploration with his father back in 1607. Then,

VOYAGE OF THE HALF MOON

John had been only ten years old — a small boy used only to run errands. Now in 1609, John was almost thirteen, and on his third voyage with his father. He was much taller and stronger. Under Colman's guidance, he had been learning to help man the ship's sails. John hoped that soon he would be considered a sailor, not a mere cabin boy.

John watched in silence as the bloody rowboat drew next to the *Half Moon*. The sailors had spent weeks exploring the coast of the New World without meeting any danger. That was why Captain Hudson had sent a handful of sailors in a small boat to explore the harbor they had found. John had begged his father to let him go with Colman and the others on their exploration. Now John understood all too well why his father had insisted he stay aboard the ship.

"Why did this happen?" John asked.

"Because they're devils, the people here," growled a familiar voice. John turned and saw

Robert Juet standing by his side. Juet, an expert sailor and veteran of many voyages, had come to join the others at the rail. His weather-beaten face was twisted with anger.

"Are they devils?" asked a quiet voice. It was James Robinson, a young sailor. "Remember—we attacked them first," he said. "Last week we raided a village and took all of their furs. If they're devils, what does that make us?"

"Don't be soft, man!" Juet snapped. "They are bloodthirsty, that's all!"

"That will be enough!" Hudson boomed. "Have you no respect for the dead?" He looked sadly into the smaller boat. By now, sailors had wrapped Colman's lifeless body in some sailing canvas. They were lifting the blood stained mass onto the deck of the *Half Moon*. "We will bury Colman properly this afternoon." Hudson said somberly.

"Aye, Captain," the sailors muttered.

Henry Hudson turned to the survivors of

the exploring party. "What did you discover?" he asked.

"The river ahead is deep," one sailor said. "A ship could easily pass through."

"The shore is lined with grass and flowers and fine trees," said another. "Sweet smells came from the shore."

"But the attack was terrible!" said another. "The people came from nowhere. We had no chance. Who knows what will happen to us as we travel up this river, surrounded by these people?"

Henry Hudson stroked his beard, lost in thought. John knew what ran through his father's mind. On all of his voyages, Henry Hudson had but one purpose. He wanted to find a sea route linking Europe and the rich lands of Asia. Whoever found this passage would be wealthy and famous.

Hudson's first two voyages had sent him looking for a passage over the North Pole. On both trips, he had been forced to turn back from the frozen waters of the Arctic. Now, on his third voyage, Hudson was commanding the *Half Moon*, a Dutch ship. For months the ship had sailed in the north. The harsh weather and icy waters there had made the crew lose hope.

Then Hudson had ordered the *Half Moon* to change bearing and set sail west for the New World. He had brought along a letter from a man named John Smith, an English colonist who believed that a large river spanned North America. It fed an open sea, and beyond that sea lay Asia, Smith claimed. Hudson decided to leave the northern seas and search for this river in the New World.

The *Half Moon* had spent most of the summer exploring the coast of the New World. At last, in early September, they had found a harbor leading to a great river. Could it be the passage that Henry Hudson had dedicated his life to finding? Hudson had sent Colman and the others to sound the river's depths.

John and the rest of the crew watched in silence as their tall, bearded captain strode to the bow of his ship. He gazed out at the beautiful harbor. It seemed to beckon to them, inviting them to explore its green, pleasant shores. Then John peered back over his own shoulder. He saw the bloody canvas wrapped around Colman's body. At last his father spoke. John's heart raced when he heard his father's words.

"We have come too far to turn back now," Hudson declared with quiet determination. "We will go on. We will not turn back."

At that moment, John knew that his father was determined to find the passage — or die in the search.

CHAPTER TWO
"The Hostages Have Escaped!"

"It's an attack!" Juet's cry shattered the still afternoon. John ran excitedly to the sound of Juet's voice. It had been three days since Colman's death. The crew of the *Half Moon* had spent these days exploring the vast harbor they had found. They were beginning their push up the river when Juet called out his shrill warning.

"Just look at 'em," Juet said, as John joined him at the railing of the ship. John saw two canoes filled with men in the water below. He gasped. The men were unlike any he had seen before.

They wore deerskin clothing over their lean muscular bodies. Most had long, black hair. But two of them had shaved one side of their heads clean, with the remaining hair pulled into a ponytail on the other side. The men were smiling, calling out in their own language. They held up large sacks. Three of the men were already climbing aboard.

"I'll get the captain!" Juet cried as he ran to the bridge.

John turned to James Robinson. "Do you think they mean to attack?" he asked.

James looked warily at the canoes. "I don't think so," he said in a low tone. "It might be they've come to trade."

A group of sailors cautiously approached the men who had climbed aboard. One of the natives held up a cloth sack. The sailors stepped back in alarm as the man's hand darted into the sack. He pulled out a large oyster.

John breathed a sigh of relief. "I guess you're right, James," he said.

"Grab them!" Juet cried as he scrambled from the bridge. He waved a pistol in the air.

"Those two have bows and arrows! I saw them!" Juet shouted as he pointed his gun in the air.

Juet's pistol went off with an ear-splitting "crack." The startled visitors jumped back. One turned and leapt off the ship. He hit the water with a splash.

"Get those two!" Juet yelled, pointing to the two other men. The men ran to the ship's rail, trying to escape by leaping into the river. But before they could jump overboard, the sailors rushed forward and grabbed them, holding them fast. John saw the canoes skim toward the shore.

"What's going on?" Henry Hudson demanded to know as he came on deck.

"These men are armed," Juet said, pulling

arrows out of a holder one of the men wore around his waist. "We were tricked," he said, tossing the arrows to the deck in disgust. "They came on board, acting friendly, as if they wanted to trade, but all along they were planning to attack us."

Hudson looked at the men. "Perhaps we should let them go," he said. "There are only two of them. They can't harm us now."

Juet peered at the men through narrow, suspicious eyes. Then he smiled. "I've got an idea," he said. "Let's hold them as hostages. That should prevent any more of these people from attacking us."

"Aye, Captain," a tall sailor added. "We don't want to end up like Colman. It's only right."

Henry Hudson stroked his beard in thought. "Perhaps it wouldn't hurt to hold onto them until we reach the end of this river," he said. "You have your hostages, Juet."

"You won't regret this, Captain," Juet called out as Hudson returned to the bridge.

John looked at the two hostages. They stood quietly on the deck, surrounded by sailors. The captives kept their faces expressionless as the sailors jabbed at their chests and pulled on their hair. But their eyes showed the terror John knew they must feel.

"DANCE, YOU DEVILS!"

It was a few days later. Juet and some other sailors had the hostages on deck. They had put bright red jackets on both of them, and were making fun of them. The sailors roared with laughter as the two hostages shuffled their feet.

John looked away, his face flushed with anger. He was on deck, cleaning fish with James Robinson.

"Father should not have let Juet take those men hostage," John said. "I suppose we can't trust these people after Colman's death. But this is just not right."

There was a sudden commotion on the deck. John turned, and was almost knocked over by Juet. "The hostages have escaped!" he shouted, rushing below deck.

John turned and saw the other sailors gathered at the side of the ship. He got to his feet and ran to join them. Juet, meanwhile, had taken a pistol from his cabin. He ran to the ship's side while he tried to load, and cursed as he fumbled with the gun.

"Don't let them get away!" Juet cried.

John looked out into the water. The two men were swimming hard, and were already halfway to shore. Soon they were on land, dripping wet, and shouting loudly at the crew in their own language.

Henry Hudson called down to the deck from the bridge. "What happened?" he asked.

"Look," John said, pointing to the men on the shore. He glanced at his father and saw Juet aiming his pistol.

"Not now, mate," Robinson said, gently lowering Juet's gun with his hand. "There is no sense in shooting now."

"Listen to them taunt us," Juet said.

"Aye, just listen," said James Robinson.

For a brief moment, John was sure he saw James Robinson smile.

CHAPTER THREE
"It Would Seem We Have Friends Here"

Two days later, John woke to the sound of river water gently lapping against the hull by his head. The bright sun filtered through the boarded-up cabin window into the cramped cabin he shared with the other sailors. Captain Hudson had ordered the window be boarded up in case of an attack. John wished they could let the sun shine in.

John climbed out of his hammock, yawned, and stretched. He walked into the narrow galley. Robert Juet sat on a wooden bench with some of the sailors, drinking beer from a pewter mug. John took a chunk of bread and a piece of salt cod from the cook and sat on a bench next to Jodicus Honius.

Jodicus was a Dutchman. Since the *Half Moon* was a Dutch ship, half its crew members were Dutch. Jodicus was there to interpret Captain Hudson's orders for the Dutch sailors.

"Good morning, Jodicus," John said through a yawn. He gnawed on his crust of bread. "Have we had any visitors while I was asleep?" John asked.

Jodicus grinned. "Didn't your mother teach you not to eat and speak at the same time?" he asked.

John swallowed his bread. "Sorry, Jodicus," he said. "It has been a long time since my mother has told me anything."

"Now, as for your question," Jodicus said, "we have had a visit this morning. An old man from a nearby village has approached the *Half Moon*. He wants your father to meet his people."

"You mean, he's going ashore?" John asked, jolting wide awake. "Did Father say that he would go?"

"No one knows," Jodicus replied.

"If he's wise, he'll not go near those killers," Juet said.

"I'm going to find out!" John said, and scrambled up on deck. His father stood at the rail, looking at the water below. John joined him. He saw a tall, white-haired man sitting in a canoe. He wore an animal skin about his waist, and a cloak decorated with white feathers hung down his back. Alongside him were two boys who didn't look much older than John.

"This man is the leader of a nearby village," Henry told John. "He wants me to come ashore."

John looked at them closely. They smiled

and nodded up at the Hudsons. Then John remembered the sight of Colman's body. He shuddered. "How can we be sure they aren't setting a trap?" he asked.

"We can't," Henry said. "But we can't travel up this river in constant fear. We must attempt to make friends with the native people." Hudson looked somber. "I'm going to accept their invitation," he said quietly.

"You can't go by yourself," John promptly said. "Take me with you."

Henry looked at his son, surprised. "Why should I risk your life as well as mine?"

"You'll need someone to scout around while you talk with the chief. I can find out if they've got weapons ready, or if they're planning an attack."

Henry stroked his beard. "You are one of the few crewmen I trust, save Juet and Jodicus. I need the two of them here to keep order in my absence," he said. Hudson smiled and placed a hand on his son's shoulder. "All right. We'll face the unknown together. You shall come along."

John's chest swelled with pride. "Thank you," he said. "I won't let you down."

Hudson sent John below deck to fetch several knives and two hatchets to be used for trading. John soon was at his father's side at the ship's rail, holding the goods in a cloth sack.

The Captain climbed down the rope ladder on the side of the ship and stepped into the canoe. John threw the sack over his shoulder and climbed down after him. The canoe bobbed under his weight as John stepped into it. He looked up at the deck of the *Half Moon*. Members of the crew peered over the rail. "God be with you," someone called in a somber voice. John could feel his heart beat within his chest. He wondered if he would ever return to the ship.

John looked from side to side as he sat in the canoe. It seemed to have been carved out of a large log. John felt it wobble, and he looked skeptically at his father. He hoped it could hold their weight. His fears disappeared as soon as the two boys began paddling with wooden oars. The craft glided smoothly away from the *Half Moon*.

John studied the two young men. They stared right back at him. *What are they thinking?* John wondered. *Are they planning to slash my throat when we are out of sight of the* Half Moon? He looked away. *I must not show any fear,* he thought.

Soon the canoe reached shallow water near the river bank. The three natives climbed out. Hudson did the same, and John followed his father's lead. As soon as his feet touched the sandy soil, John lost his balance. His legs went weak, and his knees buckled. John fell backwards into the water with a loud splash.

Henry Hudson reached down and took John's hand. "You have yet to find your land legs, son," he said, smiling.

John looked up, his cheeks burning with shame. The others were smiling at him, too.

The chief motioned for them to follow. He led John and Henry Hudson away from the shore and through a grove of trees. John glanced from side to side, half expecting arrows to rain on them from the shadows. A few hundred yards from the river, they came to a village. A crowd of people gathered as they approached. John breathed a small sigh of relief. He saw tiny children and many old people among the adults there. It was hardly likely that they all would take part in an attack. Still, John resolved to keep on his guard.

Most of the men, children, and older people wore animal skins, like the chief. The women wore skins, too, but theirs were decorated with colorful embroidery.

The crowd parted as the men led John and his father into the heart of the village. There,

John saw a large round house with an arched roof. A fire burned next to this lodge, and several women were preparing food nearby. There were three smaller round buildings next to the lodge.

The procession stopped outside of the lodge. The chief put one hand on Captain Hudson's shoulder. With the other, he motioned for them to step inside the bark dwelling. Henry looked at his son, then nodded. They entered the lodge together.

A shaft of bright sunlight poured into the building through a hole in the ceiling. Smoke from a fire in the center of the lodge rose through the sunlight and out the hole. John felt pressure from behind gently nudge him forward. He looked back and saw that the people of the village had followed them into the lodge.

The chief sat down on a mat next to the fire. He pointed to two mats on the floor near him. "We'd better sit," Henry Hudson told his son. They all sat. Henry Hudson's eyes were fixed on the chief.

John scanned the room, searching for signs of danger. He tried to look confident, but his palms were damp.

He glanced over at his father's face. Henry's expression worried John. He looked pale, and tiny drops of sweat glistened on his forehead. Henry caught John's glance, and quickly nodded his head in the chief's direction.

A bow and three arrows lay on the floor next to the chief. John glanced about him quickly, and saw that many of the other men had bows and arrows by their sides.

John's heart began to beat faster. Was this the plan, after all? Was this what happened to Colman? He felt confident, safe—and then was suddenly attacked?

The chief, a puzzled look on his face, eyed Captain Hudson. Suddenly, the old man's face brightened, and he nodded and smiled. The chief picked up his arrows and held them forward. John started with fear. Then the old chief broke the arrows in two with a loud "snap" and threw them in the fire.

The chief called out words in his own language. The other men in the lodge snapped their arrows and threw them into the fire. They gave a loud cheer.

Henry Hudson breathed a sigh of relief and turned to his son. "It would seem we have friends here," he said.

John smiled. For the first time since they had left the ship, he was at ease.

CHAPTER FOUR
"The Cry of a Wolf"

The men's cheers died down, and three women came into the lodge. Each of them carried a red wooden bowl. One of the women handed a bowl to John. A delicious odor rose from it. John's stomach rumbled.

The chief picked up a slice of flat bread from his bowl and scooped some food into his mouth. Henry and John did the same.

The food was a thick yellow pudding. John licked his lips. Fresh food was rare on their voyages. To John, this pudding was the most delicious food in the world.

His father turned to John. "It looks as though we are safe for now," he said. "I want you to learn all you can about these people while I meet with their leader. If this river is the passage we are looking for, many others will come this way soon."

"I understand," said John. "I'll find out what crops they grow and what animals they hunt."

Henry Hudson placed a cautioning hand on John's shoulder. "Don't wander off too far," he said, looking around the lodge. "We cannot afford to be entirely off guard."

"I'll look after myself," John said. Just then, the chief called out to a group of four older boys. They promptly picked up their bows and left the lodge.

"Do you think he sent them to attack the ship?" John asked, panicked. Henry patted a reassuring hand on his son's knee.

"Only four boys? I doubt it," he said. "I would wager that the boys have been sent to fetch more food," Hudson said, scooping the last of the pudding from his bowl.

John smiled. "Good," he said. "This is a nice change from stale bread, moldy cheese, and dried-out meat."

As they waited, John stood and made his way through the round lodge. The people there seemed happy, he thought. It was as though they were part of one family. The crew of the *Half Moon* had been like a family to him for many months now, but it wasn't the same. John noticed one woman about the same age as his mother back in England. He felt a pang of sadness. For the first time in a long time, John realized how much he missed his family back home.

John came to a group of large leather sacks stacked in one part of the dwelling. He looked inside and saw they were filled with dried beans and yellow grains. Although the weather was still warm, John knew winter would come soon. He guessed that these people stored food for those cold months in the same way people did back in Europe.

John heard soft laughter behind him. A small girl was standing on her toes, reaching out with one hand.

"What's so funny?" John asked, puzzled by the girl's laughter. The girl must have seen his confusion. She pointed at his head.

Suddenly, he understood. It must be my hair, John thought. After months on the open sea, his hair had become a bright golden blond. How strange it must seem to her!

He bent down. "See, it's hair, just like yours," he said. The girl reached out again and gingerly touched the top of his head. She then squealed happily and pulled her hand back. A group of children had gathered, and they laughed with her.

A tall boy stepped up to them. He took the girl's hand and said something to her. Her smile faded and she dropped her eyes to the ground

"No, no, it's all right," John said. "I don't mind." He smiled, hoping that the boy would understand.

The boy smiled back, then patted the girl on the head. She raised her eyes and her smile returned. John was thrilled. They had understood each other!

"What's your name?" John asked excitedly.

The boy looked puzzled, and John realized he had spoken without thinking. The boy had understood the expression on his face, perhaps, but not his words.

John put his hand on his own chest. "John," he said. The little girl laughed.

But a look of understanding crossed the boy's face. He laid his hand across his own chest, and said, "Etow."

"Etow," John repeated, and the boy's smile grew wider. The boy's name was Etow!

Just then, there was a commotion outside

the lodge. Etow followed as John stepped into the doorway. The young men had returned with two fat birds. Next to the lodge, several women were using oyster shells to skin the carcass of a large dead dog. Another woman took the pigeons from the hunters and began to pluck the feathers from them.

Soon the dog and pigeons were roasting on the fire outside the dwelling. Although the thought of eating a dog didn't exactly appeal to John, the smell of the meat set his stomach growling. Then he remembered the job he had to do. He hoped Etow would show him around the village.

"I wonder where they grow their crops," John thought aloud. He tried to think of a way to communicate his question to Etow. He got an idea and motioned for Etow to follow him back into the lodge. John put his hand in one of the bean sacks and let the beans flow through his fingers.

"Where do these come from?" John asked.

Etow looked puzzled for a moment. Then a look of understanding crossed his face. He nodded and led John outside. John followed Etow behind the lodge, where an astonishing sight met his eyes. Mats covered the ground outside the house, and spread out on them were thousands of yellow and brown beans.

"There are enough beans here to fill three ships!" John exclaimed. He looked at the warm sun overhead. The beans must have been put on the mats to dry, he guessed. Then the beans were stored in bags like the one John had seen inside the lodge.

Etow tugged on John's sleeve, and John followed him. They walked through the trees, and John saw a large green field ahead of them. When they were closer, John could see hundreds of mounds of earth scattered around the field. Many tall bean stalks grew out of each mound, waving in the light breeze. John had never seen anything like this field. Back in England, farmers planted crops in straight, plowed rows. Etow's people had a different way of growing things.

John followed Etow as they made their way through the bean field. In a few minutes they reached the far side, where a stream babbled over the rocky ground. Bright fish darted swiftly beneath the clear water. Etow knelt and began to drink. John did the same. The water was fresh and sweet.

Etow stood up and motioned for John to follow him farther away from the village. John regretfully shook his head. He would have liked to have seen more, but he remembered his father's warning not to wander.

"We must go back," John said, pointing in the direction of the village.

When they arrived back at the lodge, the meat was ready. All of the villagers joined in the feast.

THE MEAL LASTED SEVERAL HOURS. Besides the delicious food, there was dancing and singing unlike anything John had ever heard before. Etow stayed by his side the whole time.

When the feast was over, Henry asked John for the sack of knives and hatchets he had brought from the ship. John watched as his father traded the goods for grain and a sack of colorful beads.

After the trading, John stepped to the clearing in front of the lodge. The sun was sinking low in the sky. He sighed. John no longer felt afraid—not of the people in this village, at least. He wondered what else he and his father would find in this New World.

A mournful howl pierced the air. John shuddered. It was a sound he had often heard in England—the cry of a lonesome wolf.

Etow put a hand on John's shoulder and pointed to the lodge. Etow was pointing to a large design painted on the bark. John had noticed it before, but could not tell what it was. Now he understood.

"Wolf," John said.

"Wolf," Etow repeated.

Henry stepped outside of the lodge. "We must return to the ship, John," he said. "It will be dark soon."

John turned and grasped his new friend by the hand. "Good-bye, Etow. I hope to see you before we sail tomorrow." As before, Etow nodded, and John knew he understood.

The canoe carried John and Henry Hudson back to the *Half Moon*. The water, reflecting the setting sun, was now a deep shade of orange. The evening was quiet as they glided across the still surface. As they neared the ship, a wolf's cry filled the air once again.

John thought of his new friend Etow, and smiled.

CHAPTER FIVE
"They Have Never Seen People like Us Before"

John woke up the next morning as the first rays of sun pierced the cracks of the boarded-up window. He pulled on his boots and went to the deck. The ship had not traveled during the night. John could almost see the round lodge on the distant shore. Some of the villagers were at the water's edge, looking out at the ship.

James Robinson came up next to him. "And how was your adventure yesterday, young John?" he asked.

"It was great," John said. "We ate a big dog that the chief had killed for us."

"Dog?" James asked, hardly believing his ears. "You ate dog meat?"

John shrugged his shoulders. "It was better than that awful salted cod," he said. "The entire village joined the feast. And there is a boy there about my age. His name is Etow."

"Your father said the visit was a great success," announced a crusty old voice. It was Robert Juet. "Sounds like you foxed 'em. Now they think we're their friends. Good work, boy." John flinched as Juet rubbed his head. "Now maybe the devils will leave us in peace," Juet muttered as he ambled for the bridge.

"Come, John," James said. "Your father is sending a group of sailors ashore to shoot some of those plump birds you ate yesterday."

John and James walked to the side of the ship. John saw his father giving instructions to four sailors as they boarded the rowboat.

"I was expecting you," Captain Hudson said as James and John approached. "There is room for one slim boy in the rowboat this morning. But there are no boys on this ship, only sailors, isn't that true, John?"

John could tell that he was being teased. "I'm a boy," John said eagerly, "and a slim one, too."

"After all of that dog you ate yesterday, I'm not so sure," his father said with a laugh. "I want you to go ashore with the men. The people of this land know you. I would go myself, but I have things to do on the ship."

"I'll go," John said, climbing into the rowboat.

"Make it quick," Henry warned. "The water is high, and we must sail before noon," Henry said.

"Aye, sir," John said.

The rowboat was wider and slower than the canoe had been. It seemed as though hours instead of minutes passed before they made it to the shore. When the boat finally reached land, John sprang from the bow to the shore. This time, he kept his balance. I have my land legs now, John thought with a smile.

A crowd of people had gathered near the water's edge when the rowboat came near. They silently stared at the sailors.

"These folks give me the shakes," one sailor said, glancing around nervously.

"Don't be afraid," John said. "They won't hurt us." John looked at the faces. Where was Etow? Then he felt a hand touch his shoulder. John turned and saw his new friend. Etow smiled, and spoke some words that John did not understand. But John understood Etow's smile.

"I'm glad to be back," John said. "Come on, men, follow me."

"Well, well, look who's made himself captain," said one sailor, pushing his cap back off his brow. "Aye, aye, sir," he said, saluting sarcastically. But he and the others followed John, who led them to the village.

As they walked, John thought about what he had seen the previous day. He remembered seeing woods just beyond the bean fields. Was that where the birds could be found? John stopped and tapped Etow on the shoulder. Grabbing a twig, he knelt down and drew the outline of a bird in the sandy soil at his feet. He showed the drawing to Etow, and his friend nodded. He pulled John's arm and began to walk toward the village.

"Etow knows where the birds are," John told the sailors.

Etow and John led the men into the clearing, past the oak lodge and the drying beans, and through the bean fields. People nodded and stared as the sailors walked by. John noticed that the sailors were looking at the people with fear and nervously fingering the triggers of their guns. He remembered how he had felt just yesterday.

"It's all right," John said. "They have never seen people like us before."

Etow was saying something to him now, and pointing to the woods.

"This must be where the birds we are looking for roost," John said.

The sailors nodded. John followed Etow, who walked silently in his soft skin shoes. Brown twigs crunched under John's thick leather boots.

The day seemed to grow quieter as they traveled into the woods. The bright sun did not shine here. Instead, the branches of the tall trees formed a dark canopy above them. John recognized the towering pine trees, and the sturdy oaks whose leaves were just beginning to turn yellow. There were elm trees, he knew, and chestnuts. But there were other trees that John could not name.

John heard birds calling in the branches of the trees overhead. "I'm sure you'll find birds here," John whispered to the sailors.

"Aye," one of the men said. "We'll bag some fresh game. I'm sure. If we get separated, let's meet back in the bean field." He and another sailor walked toward a group of pines at their left.

Etow walked forward at a quick, steady pace, and John struggled to keep up. Looking behind him, he saw that they had lost the other two sailors. He wanted to tell Etow that they should turn back. But in the awesome quiet, he was afraid to make a noise.

Etow suddenly stopped. Had he seen something? John looked past him, and froze in fear.

About fifty feet ahead stood a huge gray wolf. Shaggy fur covered its body, and its piercing blue eyes seemed to be staring right through them.

John shuddered. When he was a boy in England, a wolf had attacked his mother's chickens. Henry had shot it with a pistol.

John would never forget how fierce that creature was, or how it tore the birds to bloody shreds. Is this what would happen to him? John saw that Etow had no bow and arrow. They were at the wolf's mercy.

John turned to run, but Etow firmly grabbed him by the shoulder. The boy stood perfectly still, almost as though he were no longer breathing. John tried to keep as still as his friend, but he was certain the wolf could hear his pounding heart.

The wolf turned its head. John swallowed hard. It was coming toward them, he was sure. But the wolf turned away and trotted off into the forest.

"Let's go," John said in a harsh whisper. He turned and quickly headed out of the woods.

At first, Etow did not reply. But as they walked briskly back to the field, Etow spoke excitedly. John did not understand him, but Etow seemed thrilled to have seen the wolf.

A series of loud gunshots rang through the air, and Etow jumped.

"Don't be afraid," John said. "The men must have shot some birds."

Sure enough, when they returned to the fields, the four sailors were there. They had shot six birds among them. Some of the villagers had heard the shots and had run to the field, where they cowered in fright.

"Ha!" one sailor said. "I guess they've never seen gun and powder before." Etow walked up to the man, looking at the gun with great curiosity. "Go ahead, look," the man said. "But don't touch — it's still hot."

Etow, fascinated by the musket, seemed to have forgotten all about their encounter with the wolf. John could not help but still feel frightened after their close call. What if I had run? he wondered. Would the wolf have come after me then? He thought of Etow holding him back. His friend may have saved his life.

"Time to go, John Hudson. Your father

will be waiting for us," one of the sailors called to him.

John turned to Etow. "Thank you, Etow. After we travel this river and make it to Asia, I will return," he promised. "I will see you again."

John extended his hand. Etow smiled and grasped it. As before, he knew his friend did not understand his words, but John was sure Etow knew what was in his heart.

CHAPTER SIX
"Night Is Coming"

"Not bad, eh?" James Robinson asked John as he held up a large silver fish, still flopping in the morning air. James slapped the fish to the deck of the *Half Moon* and began to cut away its gills with a sharp knife "I've never seen a river with such plentiful fish."

"There's no lack of food here, is there?" John said. He was helping Robinson and some other sailors clean the fish they had caught.

" It's much better than the blasted north-ern seas," one sailor said with a shudder. "I much prefer this green and pleasant country."

"Just think," John said, watching the beau-tiful shore as they passed up the river. "Traveling this river will make the journey to the East a pleasure, not a struggle."

Jodicus Honius looked up from the small piece of wood he was whittling. "Will it now?" he asked. Jodicus shook his head. "I'm not sure this river leads to Asia," he said.

"Don't be so gloomy," John said. "This must be the passage to the East. The river is just as John Smith described it." He sounded confident, but Jodicus's words had darkened his mood.

"Aye, but the water here is often shallow," Jodicus explained. "Remember, we have run aground once already. We may have to turn back soon."

John looked away. He did not want to listen. They could not fail a third time. They had all come so far, and worked so hard.

"Don't worry, John," James said patting him on the back. "Our journey is far from over."

"Aye, son," Jodicus said. "I don't mean for you to lose hope. None of us want to give up now." He cut a few more strokes into the wood, and handed the piece to John. "Here, a gift for you," he said.

"Thanks," John said. The Dutchman had carved a tiny replica of the *Half Moon*, sails and all. We will not fail this time, John told himself.

JOHN WORRIED FOR THE NEXT FEW DAYS about what Jodicus had said. But as time passed and the *Half Moon* continued its journey, John's spirits lifted. The sailors met with more native people as they traveled. These people, like Etow's, proved to be friendly. Soon, John had almost forgotten Jodicus's warning.

One morning, Henry Hudson sent Juet and four others upriver in the rowboat to sound out the water's depth. If the water was deep enough, they would continue. If it was shallow, they would turn back.

The day was warm, and John passed the time by fishing and swimming in the cool water. But every hour he anxiously looked up the river for signs of the rowboat. It was dark when John heard the oars splashing in the water below them, and Juet's voice booming out in the darkness.

"Good news, Captain," he said when he had climbed aboard. "The water is shallow a short distance ahead—only two fathoms deep—but we can pass it. Then the river narrows, but above that place the water is seven or eight fathoms deep. We can take the *Half Moon* farther."

"Fine," Hudson said. "We will lift anchor and sail all night."

"Hooray!" yelled John. The other sailors laughed at his enthusiasm.

The ship traveled far that night and morning, but the next afternoon the wind blew strong to the south. "We'll drop anchor here and continue tomorrow if the wind is fairer and to the north," Henry said.

John was impatient. He felt certain that they were only days away from the great sea which led to Asia. "Why do we have to stop?" he asked his father.

"I am sending Smith, the carpenter, and others ashore to cut a new yard for the foremast," his father replied. "Our foremast took a beating while we were at sea, and we should replace it while we have the chance."

John beamed. "Could I go with them?" he asked eagerly. His father smiled.

"I was just about to ask if you would," he said. "You've proved that you can communicate with the people of this land. If the crew were to encounter anyone, I'd feel better with you along."

"Thank you, sir," John said. He felt very proud of himself. He was truly a part of the crew now.

THE ROWBOAT FINALLY REACHED LAND. The shore was rockier here than near Etow's village, John saw. Smith stepped out and began to scan the trees in front of them.

"We must find a straight young pine, near forty feet high," he said, scratching his red beard.

"I'll take John into the outskirts of the woods with me," James Robinson said. "It looks like there are some young trees there. We won't go too far."

James and John made their way into the woods. Once again, John was struck by the cool quiet under the trees.

"This would make a fine foremast," John said, tapping a young tree. "She's tall and straight."

"You're right, John. Let's fetch Smith," James said.

Just as John was about to turn he saw a slight movement in the huge ferns that covered the ground under the trees. He peered ahead, then gasped. John saw the strong body and thick gray fur of a wolf. It was like the one he and Etow had seen, but this one was even closer.

"James," he whispered, "see there." His heart was beating fast, but more from excitement than fear.

James looked ahead, saw the wolf, and gulped. "Hold still, John," he said in a low, nervous voice. "I have a pistol in my belt."

"No!" John whispered. "Just wait."

The two stood breathlessly still, staring at the wolf. The wolf stared back. After a few seconds it abruptly turned and ran off into the forest.

James let out a long breath. "What a magnificent beast. I am glad I was not forced to kill it," he said. "You act as though you have met a wolf before."

"I have," John said, "with Etow. He taught me to stand still."

"Your friend must know these animals well," James said. "Perhaps they will not attack us unless we attack them first."

John suddenly shivered. The air seemed to have grown cold. "Let us go find Smith," he said, still whispering. "I'm afraid night is coming."

"Aye," James said, and they left the woods.

DARKNESS WAS FALLING before Smith and the others had the foremast ready. When they returned to the ship, John saw that a group of natives had come on board. They were eating with the rest of the crew. John, James, and the others joined in.

The next day, the people returned to the ship at noon. Six men and four women came aboard with gifts of tobacco and beads. John fingered the cool, smooth strands. The beads were brightly colored—blue, purple, red, and white. His mother would like them, he thought.

At noon, Hudson sent Juet and four others upriver to sound out the water's depth. The rest of the crew joined in another feast with the natives.

"The crew seems happy today," John told his father.

"Yes," Henry said, but his face looked worried. "I hope their mood lasts. I pray we will hear good news when Juet returns."

A cold chill ran down John's spine.

"We won't have to turn back, will we?" he asked. "This river is wide and deep. It must be the passage we have been searching for."

Henry Hudson shook his head. "I am not as confident as you," he replied. "I hoped we would have come to the sea by now. Or at least found some sign that we were approaching it. Instead the river grows narrower and narrower." Henry Hudson saw the crestfallen expression on his son's face, then smiled. "Perhaps I should try to share your enthusiasm," he said. "Yes, we must have hope!"

John tried to forget his father's fears, but they hung about him the rest of the day like a dark cloud. John anxiously watched the river, waiting for Juet's return.

Night came, and a soft rain began to fall. There was still no sign of the rowboat. John went below deck and climbed into his hammock. I must have hope, he told himself as he tried to fall asleep. I must have hope.

He slept lightly, and was soon awakened by low voices and footsteps on deck. He walked above, and found most of the crew gathered on deck. Juet had returned.

The first mate was talking in low tones with the captain. John shivered as the cold raindrops fell on his head. He felt a growing sense of dread.

"What is the word, Captain?" Jodicus

asked. "The Dutch sailors are in a restless mood. I must tell them our plans. Will we sail farther up the river?"

John held his breath. The moon came from behind a bank of dark clouds, and a thin ray of silver moonlight illuminated Henry Hudson's face. John knew from his father's expression what the answer would be.

"The water is too shallow," Henry said. His voice was steady. "There is but seven feet of water ahead. We must turn back. This is not the passage we are seeking."

I must be asleep still, John thought. Perhaps this is a dream. But the low whispers of the crew were real enough. Jodicus translated Henry's words for the Dutch sailors, and their angry muttering hung heavily in the air. John knew no one would dare to speak openly against his father. To do so could mean punishment by whipping, or even death.

"It was wise to come to this place," Jodicus spoke. "I stand by our decision."

"Aye!" a few of the sailors added, but their voices were half-hearted.

"Everyone should try to rest," Henry said. "We will begin our journey home in the morning."

John watched his father walk back to his cabin. His head was bowed. Three times he had searched for a passage to Asia. Three times he had failed. They would return to Europe beaten, not proud.

One by one, the sailors went below deck. The moon disappeared behind the clouds, and more rain began to fall. John stood quietly in the wet night. He stayed on deck until the last man had gone, watching the raindrops splash into the dark river below.

CHAPTER SEVEN
"This Man Does Not Deserve to Die!"

"What's wrong, Father?" John asked. It was a few days after the *Half Moon* had turned and begun to sail down the river toward the ocean. The mood on the ship had been tense. John knew from the lines on his father's face that something was wrong.

"It's the crew," Henry said, looking over his shoulder to make sure no one could overhear. "I'm not sure that I can trust them. I think that I am losing control of them."

As if on cue, an angry cry burst from the bow of the ship. Captain Hudson hurried toward the noise.

John ran behind his father. A crowd of men were gathered in a circle. A tall, muscular sailor was screaming in Dutch at Juet, whose scowl was worse than ever. Jodicus Honius stood between them.

"Juet! What is going on?" Henry shouted.

"It's these Dutch rascals, Captain! They will not do their share of the work."

"Jodicus, is this true?" Henry asked, turning to Honius.

"I cannot say, Captain," Jodicus said. "The men were already fighting when I got there. Petyr claims he cannot work with this rude Englishman. He also says they don't know why they should work when the voyage has failed."

Henry's face reddened. "Tell those Dutch scoundrels that as long as they are sailors on the *Half Moon*, they will follow orders! That goes for everyone aboard!" he added, eyeing Juet. "With luck, and if everyone does his share, we should be home in less than two months."

"Aye, Captain," Jodicus said. He turned to a group of sailors and spoke to them in Dutch. The men grumbled, but returned to their stations.

"Get back to work!" Henry Hudson shouted, his words directed at the English sailors who had gathered behind Juet. John remained by his father's side as the sailors walked away.

The Hudsons stood alone at the center of the deck. Henry sighed deeply.

"I've let our sponsors down," he said. "They sent me north to find a passage to Asia. What have I done? Defied orders — come to this river—"

"And it's a beautiful place," John interrupted. "Maybe they will think our discoveries here are almost as valuable as a shortcut to Asia."

"I hope so," Henry Hudson said. "Because I will need all of their good graces if I hope to raise money for a fourth voyage."

"A fourth voyage?" John echoed in surprise.

"Yes," Henry said. He smiled at his son. "You didn't think we were giving up, did you? No, and we never will. On this voyage, we have proved that this river is not the passage. But that passage exists. I know it does." Hudson looked down at the water lapping against the ship's hull. "And I will be the one to find it. I know I will."

THE *HALF MOON* SAILED ALL DAY AND NIGHT and anchored at noon the next day. The river was wider, and John knew that they were nearing the ocean. Soon, he would say good-bye to the New World — perhaps forever. When James and some of the crew were sent ashore to gather ripe chestnuts, John asked to go with them.

In a few hours, their sacks were full and they returned to the *Half Moon*. When they approached the ship, John noticed three birch-bark canoes alongside her.

"Father must have allowed some people aboard to trade," John said. Climbing aboard, he saw several men trading furs with his father, Jodicus, and some of the crew. Juet stood at the stern, staring into the water below.

"What do you think old Juet is up to?" John asked James.

"Who knows?" the sailor replied. "Let's find out."

John nodded, and the two walked to the stern. Juet must have heard them approach, since he looked up.

"What are you doing here? I thought you would be fawning over your savage friends," Juet said.

"This Man Does Not Deserve to Die!"

"We thought we would join you, friend," James said sarcastically. "It seems there is something of great interest in the water below."

"Aye," Juet said, lowering his voice to a harsh whisper. "Just see for yourself."

John looked over the stern. Below them, a young man sat quietly in a canoe.

"What is he doing?" John asked.

"Plotting to slit out throats, no doubt," Juet said. "But he won't succeed, not if I can help it."

James shook his head. "Juet, you are far too suspicious. These people have shown us nothing but kindness these past few weeks."

"It's a trick," Juet said. "Have you forgotten how they killed Colman? They're all up to no good, like that scoundrel down there." He pointed down below, and his eyes grew wide. "He's vanished! Slipped into our cabins through the window, no doubt!" Like a shot, Juet ran and scrambled below deck. John looked at James and sighed.

"Juet assumes everyone is as nasty as he is," John said. "Let's stop him before he hurts someone."

John and James ran after the old sailor. John reached the short ladder that led below deck. He put his feet on the rungs, but someone grabbed his ankle and tugged. John lost his balance, fell, and hit the floor with a thud. Looking up, he saw the young native hurrying up the ladder. The young man was peering back over his shoulder, a terrified look on his face.

"We won't hurt you," John told him. But the man didn't seem to hear.

John turned and saw Juet hurrying down the narrow passageway, loading his pistol. James Robinson scrambled down the ladder and confronted Juet.

"Stop that thief!" Juet cried. "I found him in my cabin. I caught him stealing two of my shirts and a pillow. No one steals from Robert

Juet and lives!"

James grabbed him. "Don't be crazy! This man does not deserve to die!"

"Let me pass!" Juet screamed. The two sailors struggled. James tried to take the gun from Juet. Juet raised the gun and brought its barrel down onto James's head with a loud crack. James slid to the floor.

"James!" John Hudson cried, crawling to his friend's side as Juet climbed above deck. "Are you hurt?" he asked. Blood oozed from a cut on James's head, and his eyes were closed. The blow had knocked him unconscious.

John heard a loud roar above him. "Thief!" a voice yelled.

John's heart leapt in terror as he realized that Juet was going to shoot the man. He grabbed the ladder and began to climb.

Boom!

The shock of Juet's pistol shot sent John reeling backward, but he held onto the ladder.

Terrible screams pierced the air, and when John emerged on deck, he saw the young man's body flying backward over the rail and into the water below.

"No!" John cried. Looking up, he saw his father standing behind Juet.

The men who had been trading on deck stood motionless for a second, then quickly sprang into action. They leapt over the side of the boat and swam to their canoes.

"Stop them!" Juet cried, waving his smoking gun in the air.

A cheer went up among the sailors on deck. A few grabbed their pistols from their gun belts and climbed into the rowboat.

"No one has permission to leave this ship!" Henry Hudson roared at the men.

But it was too late. Juet and the sailors were already in the boat, rowing furiously after the canoes.

CHAPTER EIGHT
"I Will Miss This Land"

"Father, stop them!" John called as he ran to the railing of the ship.

Henry shook his head. "I'm sorry. The men have taken matters into their own hands. There is nothing I can do to stop them now."

John watched as the three canoes sped away from the rowboat. He felt relieved—the canoes were so light and swift that the sailors would never catch them. Within minutes, the canoes had outdistanced the rowboat by a good fifty yards. Some of the sailors fired shots which splashed in the water far short of the canoes.

But then, a loud cry rose from the rowboat. John strained to see what was happening. One of the natives was trying to climb aboard the rowboat!

John saw the ship's cook pull a sword from his belt and lift it above the struggling man. John shut his eyes, and turned away. But he could not drown out the man's cries of pain.

John looked at the rowboat. The native man was out of sight, but the cook was waving his bloody sword as the other sailors cheered. John dropped to his knees, his stomach churning.

"Are you all right, son?" Hudson asked.

"Yes," John replied weakly. Then, he remembered James. "James Robinson is hurt, Father. Juet hit him."

"Go help him, son. I will attend to matters here. The crew's attack is sure to anger the people all along this shore. We must leave the river as quickly as possible," Henry said.

John climbed below deck. James was sitting up, and his eyes were open. He was holding his hand over the bloody lump that had formed on his head.

"What happened, John?" James asked.

"Juet shot the man who he found in his cabin," John said. "The other natives left the ship, and Juet and some of the crew gave chase. The cook killed one with his sword."

"The fools!" James said.

"Will you be all right?" John asked, helping James to his feet.

"I think so," James said. "I'd better be. We'll need all hands working to make it back to sea as quickly as possible. I'm sure we'll be attacked."

John helped James above deck. The rowboat was returning to the ship. The sailors cheered and patted the cook on the back.

"Good work," one of the sailors said. "It's

a shame we didn't kill more."

Henry approached Juet. He should punish them all, John thought with anger. But he knew how foolish that would be. To challenge the will of the crew at this point could mean mutiny.

"Hoist the sails! There will be no rest for anyone until we reach the ocean!" Captain Hudson ordered. He pointed to one of the sailors. "Christopher, man the lookout. Our lives are in danger until we are back at sea."

DESPITE JOHN'S PROTESTS, Henry Hudson made his son stay below deck. John tossed in his hammock that night as the *Half Moon* sailed speedily down river. But to John it didn't seem fast enough. He knew the large ship could not outrace the natives' sleek canoes.

The night seemed unusually quiet. But John could not sleep. Was the ship about to be attacked? Would he be killed by an arrow through his heart?

John sat upright. The first light of day filtered through the window into the cabin. He had fallen asleep after all. John jumped from his hammock — then stopped.

The *Half Moon* was silent.

For one terrifying moment, John feared that he was alone on the ship. What if all of the crew had been killed during the night? Panic-stricken, John scrambled above deck. He breathed a sigh of relief when he saw his father, Juet, and the rest of the crew standing silently at the stern.

John joined them, then gasped. Off in the distance were two large canoes. Each was filled with men, their angry faces covered with bright paint. They stared silently at the *Half Moon*.

"Now it begins," Henry said. He noticed his son standing at his side. "John! Return to your quarters. At once!"

"But Father," John protested. "I can't hide

like a baby, not when we are fighting for our lives!"

"Don't argue. Get below deck, now!" Henry ordered.

"Captain!" Juet called. "Here they come!"

Hudson turned his attention to the river. The canoes were nearing. From this distance, John could see that their pursuers fitting arrows against the drawstrings of their bows.

John looked across the deck and saw that most of the crew had taken positions along the boat's rail, their pistols poised. Juet was manning a falcon, a large gun that looked like a small cannon.

John couldn't hide and leave them to fight. Then he saw it. One of the sailors had left a pistol propped against a coil of rope behind him, loaded and ready to fire once he had shot the two pistols he already held. John crept over behind the sailor, silently snatched the pistol, and took a position at the rail next to Juet.

The men in the canoes were yelling now — a loud, rhythmic, eerie cry. They had drawn much closer.

John tightly gripped the pistol, his finger on the trigger. He knew he should obey his father's orders and go below deck. And he hated the thought of using a gun. But he was almost a man. He would not hide below like a child.

"They are attacking!" a sailor shouted.

John flinched as dozens of arrows flew through the air. All thudded harmlessly against the ship's hull. Then the air exploded with the deafening sound of Juet's falcon. John watched in horror as one of the men in the canoes screamed, his midsection exploding in a shower of red. He doubled over, contorted in pain, and fell into the water with a splash.

Another volley of arrows flew through the air. One or two clattered to the deck, but no sailors were hit.

The falcon boomed again, and John heard another scream as a man fell, bleeding, to the bottom of a canoe. Two men had been killed, yet their arrows had hurt none of the crew.

"I need more ammunition!" Juet cried as the shocked men struggled to turn their canoes in the water.

The image of the young man falling from his canoe raced in John's mind. *That man wasn't much older than Etow*, John thought. Etow and his people had treated John with kindness. Etow had probably even saved his life. Yet the crew was treating them like an enemy. To John, they had only been friends.

"Hold your fire!" Captain Hudson shouted. "They are retreating!"

John looked back at the water. By now the two canoes had turned around and were speeding back to shore. John breathed a sigh of relief.

"We must kill them all before they return!" Juet cried. He turned and grabbed

John roughly by the shoulder. "Give me that, boy!" Juet snapped, snatching the pistol from John's grasp. John stumbled, caught himself, and watched dumfounded as Juet took careful aim at the departing canoes.

"Enough!" John cried. He found his balance and, with all of his might, pushed Juet aside. The pistol went off as Juet stumbled over, the shot splashing harmlessly in the water between the retreating canoes.

"You young troublemaker!" Juet cried. He regained his balance and grabbed John by the shoulders.

"Let him go!" a powerful voice demanded. Juet looked up. The look of fury and hate melted from his face before the commanding presence of Henry Hudson.

"Aye, Captain," Juet muttered. A rough hand took hold of John's shoulder, pulling him back. It was his father.

"As for you," Hudson said, looking at John with flashing eyes. "I told you to go below deck!"

"I know, sir," John said. "But I couldn't leave you and the others. Our ship was under attack. And when you are attacked, you must defend yourself."

Hudson turned and looked sadly at the water. The natives had made it to the shore, and were dragging the dead man from the canoe.

"I know that, son," Hudson said softly. "I know that all too well."

THE *HALF MOON* CONTINUED ITS COURSE without being attacked again. Within days, she reached the magnificent harbor at the mouth of the river. The wide, clear blue ocean was in sight beyond it.

Night was falling as the ship made its way out to the open sea. John stood at the ship's stern. The stiff ocean breeze roared in his ears as he watched the shore grow smaller and smaller on the horizon. Behind him, some of the Dutch sailors were whistling a tune. Jodicus was teaching an English sailor to play his wooden whistle. John sighed as the sun sank toward the beautiful and distant shore.

"I will miss this land." John turned. James Robinson stood beside him.

"I will, too," John agreed. "Perhaps we will return here some day, after we find the passage to Asia."

James smiled sadly. "I would like to," he said. "But I don't think the people of this land would welcome our return."

A strange, faint sound carried over the waves. Goose bumps sprung up on John's arms, and he shivered.

It was the mournful cry of a wolf.

"Perhaps you are right," John said quietly. "Perhaps you are right."

*John and
Henry Hudson
set adrift in
Hudson Bay*

In November, 1609, the **Half Moon**
returned to England. Henry Hudson was
certain that he could find the passage to
Asia if given just one more chance.

A group of Englishmen agreed to pay for
a fourth voyage. In 1610, Hudson set sail in
an English ship, the *Discovery*. He took his
son John with him again. And Robert Juet

was hired as first mate, despite the trouble he had caused on the voyage of the *Half Moon*.

Hudson sailed the *Discovery* to Greenland, then to the frozen waters north of Canada. He discovered the huge body of water that now bears his name: Hudson Bay. As the *Discovery* searched the vast bay for the northwest passage, it became trapped in ice. The crew spent many months in the bitter cold and near starvation.

In June of 1611, the ship broke free of the ice. But it was too late for Henry Hudson. Robert Juet led a mutiny against the captain. Juet and the crew set Henry and John Hudson, and seven others adrift in a boat with no food or water. Hudson and the others were never heard from again.

The *Discovery* reached England two months later with only a skeleton crew. Some sailors had died in conflicts with native North Americans. Many others,

A modern replica of the Half Moon sails up the Hudson River. As famous as the Half Moon is, no one knows for sure what the ship looked like. This replica is based on the New Netherlands Museum's research

including Robert Juet, starved to death on the long voyage home.

More about . . .

This book is based on fact. Henry Hudson and his crew were the first Europeans to explore the Hudson River. And Hudson's son, John, really did join him on four of his voyages. We know the details of the voyage of the *Half Moon* from diaries kept by Henry Hudson and Robert Juet.

The only part of the book that was made up is the friendship of John Hudson and Etow. But Hudson's diary does tell that Etow's people, the Mahicans, were friendly. The description of the feast where the Mahicans broke their arrows is based on Hudson's eyewitness report. Here is more information about interesting details in the book:

VOYAGE OF THE HALF MOON

Henry Hudson

Henry Hudson is one of the most mysterious figures in history. Almost nothing is known about his life before his first search for a passage to Asia in 1607. The fact that Hudson kept a diary shows that he probably went to school as a child. (In Hudson's day, usually only boys went to school. The school day lasted from seven in the morning until five at night, with a two-hour lunch break.)

No one knows when Henry Hudson first went to sea. But we do know that by 1607 he was considered an outstanding sea captain. That was the year he decided to search for a passage to Asia. He went to the Muscovy Company, a trading company in England, to ask for money for the voyage. In the minutes of the meeting, Hudson is described as "an experienced seapilot . . . who has in his possession secret information that will

Photograph of Diorama: Henry Hudson and crew aboard the Half Moon

In this model of the Half Moon, made by Dwight Franklin, the crew are looking over the rail at land. The sailors are shown in typical clothes of the period.

enable him to find the . . . passage."

Hudson didn't really have secret information. Back in 1527, a man named Robert Thorne got the idea that there was a northern waterway that led to Asia. Thorne's ideas were published in 1599. That was the "secret information" that Hudson had.

Strange Sights

In the 1600s, most people thought that

mermaids existed. Henry Hudson was no exception. In fact, he and his crew believed they saw one on the second voyage, in arctic waters. Hudson wrote in his diary, " . . . her body [is] as big as one of us, her skin very white, and her long hair, hanging down behind, of color black; in her going down they saw her tail, which was like the tail of a porpoise speckled like a mackerel."

It sounds convincing. But experts today say that Hudson and his men actually saw a walrus!

"New Amsterdam"

The Dutch East India Company may have been disappointed by Hudson's failure to find the Northwest Passage. But they were excited by his reports of the land around the river he explored. Lured by the promise of rich, green land and abundant furs, many Dutch settlers came to the area we now call New York and the waterway we call the Hudson River.

In 1612, the Dutch set up a fur trading center on the island of Manhattan. In 1626, Peter Minuit, director of the Dutch colony, "bought" the island from the Manahat Indians who lived there for 60 Dutch guilders. (That would be about $24 in today's money.) The city the Dutch founded was called "New Amsterdam." Later, the British would call the city "New York."

The Mahicans

The character Etow was a member of the Mahican Indian nation. The Indian word "mahican" translates to "wolf" in English.

Sadly, most of the Mahican people had died by the early 1700s, due to fights with Europeans and other Indian people. A small group of Mahicans survived and moved to Massachusetts. But in 1822 the United States government forced them to move to Wisconsin.

"The Northwest Passage"

Why did Henry Hudson spend so many years of his life in search of a passage to Asia? Ever since the 1200s, Europeans had traded with China. The goods from that land—spices, silk, tea, and precious metals—were in great demand. Traders made a lot of money. In Hudson's day, the voyage to China and back took three years! Whoever could find a shortcut would become rich and famous.

By the way, there really is a "Northwest Passage" north of Canada. But it is blocked by ice for most of the year. The first successful trip through the passage was made in 1906, more than three hundred years after the voyage of the *Half Moon*.

**To Learn More about
John and Henry Hudson, read . . .**

Baker, Susan, *Explorers of North America* [Austin: Steck-Vaughn, 1990]

Brown, Warren, *The Search for the Northwest Passage* [New York: Chelsea House, 1991]

Harley, Ruth, *Henry Hudson* [Mahwah: Troll Associates, 1979]

Joseph, Joan, *Henry Hudson* [New York: Franklin Watts, Inc., 1974]

Other Books in the STORIES OF THE STATES series

Drums at Saratoga*
American Dreams *
by Lisa Banim

Golden Quest*
East Side Story*
by Bonnie Bader

Fire in the Valley
Mr. Peale's Bones
by Tracey West

Forbidden Friendship
by Judith Eichler Weber

Children of Flight Pedro Pan
by Maria Armengol Acierno

*Available in paperback

If you are interested in ordering other STORIES OF
THE STATES books, please call Silver Moon Press at
our **toll free** number (800) 874-3320 or send an order to:

Silver Moon Press
126 Fifth Avenue, Suite 803
New York, N.Y. 10011

All hardcovers are $12.95 and all paperbacks are
$4.95.(Please add $1.00/ book for shipping up to a maximum of
$3.00)